C901269353

D0229089

libraries ni

You can renew your book at any library or online at
www.librariesni.org.uk

If you require help please email - enquiries@librariesni.org.uk

One morning Pom Pom got out of bed
on the **wrong** side.

POM POM
gets the grumps

PUFFIN

by
Sophy Henn

And then **nothing** was right.

His blanky, Timmington, couldn't be found.

Anywhere.

"Harrumph!" said Pom Pom.

His baby brother, Boo Boo,
    was playing with his favourite toy.

BANG! BANG! BANG!

Pom Pom's mummy sang silly, soppy songs
all through breakfast.

His cereal was soggy and
there were bits in his juice.

"Harrumph!" said Pom Pom.

Then things went from bad to worse . . .

His toothbrush was
too scratchy.

His flannel was just
freeeeeezing.

And he couldn't do
a thing with his hair.

"Harrumph!"
said Pom Pom.

After all that,
it was time to go.

Outside the sun was **too** sunny.

And the birds
were **too** noisy.

"Harrumph!"
said Pom Pom.

"Have a **lovely** day, dear,"
said Pom Pom's mummy.

"Harrumph!"
said Pom Pom.

In the playground
everyone was having fun.

Except
Pom Pom.

"Fancy a kickabout?"
asked Buddy.

"NO."
huffed Pom Pom.

"Want to watch ants?"
asked Rocco.

"NO."
grumbled Pom Pom.

"Would you like to play catch?"
asked Baxter.

"NO!"
shouted Pom Pom.

"Do you want to do skipping?"
asked Scout.

"G
AW

O
AY!"
yelled
Pom Pom.

And they did.

"oh."

Pom Pom didn't feel like shouting any more.
He felt sad. And a bit silly.
His friends had only tried to be nice.

"Oops,"
said Pom Pom.

And off he went to find the others.

"Sorry, everyone," said Pom Pom.

"That's OK,"
said everyone.

"I know," said Baxter.
"Let's play chase!"

"I'll be chaser,"
said Buddy.

"Yay!" said everyone.

"Got you!" said Buddy.

"Harrumph!"
said Pom Pom.